The Urban Goddess

JESSICA ASHBY

Semillas Publishing

Copyright © 2017 Jessica Ashby

Published by Semillas Publishing, New York, New York
www.semillaspublishing.com

Semillas Publishing is a registered trademark.

Printed in the United States of America

Design by Semillas Publishing

ISBN: 978-0-692-98245-7

THE URBAN GODDESS

CONTENTS

CONTENTS

*

CONTENTS

CHAPTER 1
HECATE AND PERSEPHONE

The city is filled with the sound of sirens. The neon lights of the grungy shopping centers reflect off the faces of scantily clad women that walk along the boulevard. The city is bustling. It smells of Chinese takeout and the stargazer lilies that line the highway. And amidst the chaos of this broken city are two girls. One is a dark-haired angel goddess. A mighty Hecate within her own mind, she was dark and sometimes secretive. Her hazel eyes glowing against the ebony night. Delilah was the day to her night. Ying and Yang. Flowing blonde hair with green eyes, her skin as pale as a water lily. A modern-day Persephone, she was naïve and hardened. Jade and Delilah. Two opposites that attracted the neighborhood boys with their mischievous smiles and criminal records, but came together to form a bond that would stand against all odds.

She was new. I had grown up with the same kids since kindergarten, so I always recognized the unfamiliar faces that trudged along the hallways. She was naturally beautiful although her eyes were adorned with light blue glitter. Her hair falling around her as she watched the bubbly personalities that had been annoying me since freshman year, I knew she was different. I had never been popular.

The few friends from middle school were now moving onto different cliques, and I was still here, waiting for someone who understood the life I lived. We were less fortunate than a lot of our classmates, and the smells of an alcoholic father entered the room before he did. Mama left him during freshman year, but he still tormented us with his presence from time to time.

Well developed at an early age, I was used to the prowling eyes of boys. The same boys who stared at your tits as you sat across from them, but looked past you in the hallways as they made their way to the enthusiastic girls in their cheerleading uniforms. I approach her skeptically.

"I really like your makeup," I tell her.

She looked up from her book, and I could see the speckles of yellow in her eyes.

"Really? Thanks." She smiles.

"Definitely. Very celestial. A modern-day fairy."

"That's kind of what I was going for. Although it doesn't seem to fit in around here," she says.

I look around at the Abercrombie and Fitch bodies walking around with their Gap hoodies and monogrammed backpacks. Preppy world. Here I was with my winged eyeliner and red lips. We stood out like two sore thumbs.

"I like that though. Normal is overrated," I say.

We sat through the rest of lunch going over her schedule. We had four classes together, and we lived on the same block of small, brick apartments that were surrounded by rows of pine trees. After school, we holed up in my tiny bedroom and listened to music. Amethyst walls adorned with pictures of Greek goddesses with their gauzy dresses and flowing locks. Quotes from my favorite authors written in lipstick and flower petals spread along my vanity, my room was my sanctuary. I sat along my black comforter as we talked about our lives. Her mother, Cherie, was divorced. They lived with her boyfriend and her younger sister. Her mother was mostly absent and sometimes neglectful, so Delilah spent most of her days alone.

"What do you do when it gets overwhelming?" she asks.

"I write. Mostly supernatural stories," I confess.

I pull out the thick binder of papers that harbored that stories of my mind. Until today, no one knew about my writing.

"I've never shown these to anyone. I sometimes think they are too fucked up for anyone to understand."

She's already engrossed in one of my stories about a girl who contracts HIV from prostituting herself.

2

"These are so good!" she squeals.

"I love to paint. I've entered a few contests, but never won anything," she tells me.

She hands me a frayed folder with the word "Private" sprawled across the top. Inside were sketches of women with dark, stringy hair and tears in their eyes. Alien-like creatures with green skin and stiletto heels. A chameleon fairy with cuts along her arms and legs. There were no words. Her work was exquisite. She looks at me timidly. "Screwed up huh?" she asks.

"No. It's amazing. I've never seen anything quite like this before," I say.

I don't remember how long we sat there…admiring each other's darkened minds and the visions it created.

CHAPTER 2
ANDROMEDA

The next day at school, I found Delilah at my favorite bench right outside the cafeteria. Her long, maxi dress flowing in the breeze and there were daisies pinned inside her long braid. My urban gypsy friend.

"I have an idea." I meant to whisper, but it came out more like a high-pitched scream.

"Really? What?" She was paying more attention to my stiletto booties and less of what I was saying.

"Delilah! Seriously," I say exasperated.

"Sorry. Tell me." She grins.

"So... I have a project idea that I think we should work on. With my writing and your art, I think we could be amazing. Create a character that has never been written about. Or drew about. Let's create her. We'll send it to every major publisher we can find. And maybe...we could find someone who doesn't think we're crazy. Someone that doesn't judge us by our works of art."

"Do you really think we could, do it? I'm a little scared of what people might think."

"You have to take chances. We're never going to get out of this place unless we try," I preach.

As she closes her eyes, I can see her lips moving ever so slowly. Then she smiles.

"Okay."

We skip our afternoon classes and head home to pack. "We need inspiration," I told her.

After a bit of pleading to my mother, and a note left for Delilah's, we headed west into the mountains. I've always loved the beach, but there's just something mysterious about the mountains. The snow. The quiet. Staring off into the pale abyss, my visions are running wild. We rented a room at a local hotel, embellished with brick fireplaces and flannel bed sheets.

"It's so cozy here!" Delilah says as she tosses her backpack on the bed.

"Come on…let's go downtown to the café and people watch." I pry her away from the snow-packed windows. Armed with fake IDs we bought from our friend, Dave, we order peppermint schnapps hot chocolates and bagels.

"Okay, so let's figure out what kind of girl we want."

"I love her hair." Delilah points out to the redhead at the bar.

"Hmm…reds good. But more like a burgundy red. She needs to be unique."

"Like a beautiful, damaged creature with red hair and blue eyes. And she paints murals of the realms she visits while sleeping," Delilah chimes in.

I turn to her and just stare.

"What? No good?" she asks.

"No…actually it's perfect," I tell her.

That was the day we created Andromeda and the beginning of turmoil that would become our lives.

CHAPTER 3
PAPER DREAMS

Over the next month, we worked every day. Periodically skipping school, we would take impromptu road trips to feed our imaginations. Beach trips that inspired water realms with seashell clad mermaids and coral reef mazes. The darker part of the city that created the secret worlds where bloodthirsty werewolves prowled about. Witches dancing naked under the full moon. Their long, dark hair lit up by the fire that surrounds them, all while they chant their spells, swaying their bodies side to side.

"I'm so excited!" Delilah squeals as she squeezes my arm.

Months of planning, writing, and digging into the deepest parts of our minds have brought us to this moment. Ten copies of our manuscript sealed and ready to mail out to different publishers across the U.S. Holding hands in our private séance, we say a quick prayer before dropping them into the mailbox.

"It's done," I say.

"How long do you think it will be before we hear anything?" she asks me.

"Not sure. It can take months… or we might not hear anything at all."

The look of defeat is on her face, and I decide that positivity is the better route of passage now. We celebrate with Chinese takeout and our favorite movies. Slurping lo mein noodles with our chopsticks as we gaze upon the beauty of Audrey Hepburn with her little black dress and dream apartment. Not expecting to hear any news for at least a few months, I was giddy and nervous when a brown manila envelope arrived in my name two weeks later. Pounding on Delilah's front door, I can hear her running through the house screaming "What?! What is it?! Are you okay?!"

Holding her chest, she frowns down at me. "You almost gave me a heart attack."

"Look what came in the mail!" I hold up the envelope.

"Is it from a publishing company?" she asks.

"Yes. They are the ones based in New York. Our top pick." I wink.

"Okay… you open it. I can't look," she says closing her eyes.

Trying to hide my shaking hands I tell her not to get her hopes up. I open the envelope and read.

Dear prospective authors,

After reviewing your manuscript "The Urban Goddess," we are pleased to announce that we would like to work with you in furthering your book. Please respond at your earliest convenience to set up a time with our publishing consultants and editors. We are excited about this new adventure!"

Sincerely,

Edward Johnston

"Oh, my God! We did it!" We chant over and over, tears are flowing from Delilah's eyes.

"Maybe we can actually get out of here now. Make something for ourselves," she says.

"We're already on our way."

CHAPTER 4
MANHATTAN

One week later, after many negotiations and phone calls, Delilah and I are side by side as we ascend into the air. Having never flown before, I gave her the window seat. I don't think her eyes ever left that window. She had that goofy grin on her face as she squeezed my hand periodically from the turbulence below.

We landed in New York at 10 AM. A limousine was waiting to take us directly to the publishing company. We slid into the leather seats feeling like a celebrity on her way to the red carpet. To say New York was amazing would be an understatement. Rows of buildings that glistened against the sun. Crowds of people bustling through the city with their chaotic lives and shopping bags. New York City reminded me of a young woman, with her onyx hair and stiletto heels. Braving the city with her stone-faced expressions to keep prowlers at bay. At night, her face would soften as she cuddled up in her small Manhattan apartment with a bottle of red and stacks of fashion magazines.

We pull up to a tall building with glass windows as far as you could see. Inside were marble floors, and pictures of famous authors that lined the lobby as if welcoming you into their world. A young, blonde woman escorted us into an office with a huge oval desk in the center of the room. There were pictures of a middle-aged man and his family with their fake smiles and artificial scenery. Stacks of manuscripts were piled on each side of the desk.

He walks in smiling. Adorned with a grey, Armani suit, he is impeccable. His dark hair combed neatly to the side. He extends his hand and introduces himself. "Edward Johnston," he says. "I'll be working directly with you and your editor."

"Delilah," she squeaks as she shakes his hand.

"Hi, I'm Jade." I look him directly in the eye and shake firmly.

"Okay, so. We love the piece. Very eclectic. Very urban. And very dark," he says. "A lot of books nowadays are too cookie cutter. Always a happy ending. Too many people are afraid to write darker stories because they fear the criticism. This is bold." He smiles.
"That was exactly what we were going for," I tell him.

"Well, it's definitely something we are interested in creating. I don't think there needs to be much change within the stories. We will have our editors review everything one last time for grammatical errors, etc. We will get you a copyright of everything once reviews are completed, and we can meet with the illustrator to intertwine Delilah's paintings to your stories." he explains.

Delilah is just sitting there grinning from ear to ear and nodding her head. Three hours' worth of interviews later, we had met with our editor, Sharon and a group of illustrators who took copies of Delilah's work. Overwhelmed and exhausted, I was so ready to get to our hotel and unwind.

CHAPTER 5
EDWARD JOHNSTON

This is going be big. I can always tell. I've been in this business long enough to see talent when it walks in the door. Always thriving, and dressed to impress, I take business seriously. I wear nothing but the best. You want to appear friendly, but powerful. Beautiful girls, especially that Jade. That long, dark hair and her pretty bangin' body too. I've always liked them young. There was something innocent about her friend, Delilah. Made you wonder if she could ever be bad. I sometimes feel like a shitty husband because I fuck other women, but after twenty years of being married to a frigid bitch whose idea of a good time is a Tupperware party, you must find an outlet. We'll just have to see how it goes.

CHAPTER 6
HOME "SWEET" HOME

Delilah flops on the pillow top mattress, and she sinks into the white comforter. "This room is so beautiful. I don't think we have hotels like this back at home." Dinner was exquisite. Thai noodles in ginger sauce with skewers of chicken and vegetables. Ornately positioned, we devoured molten chocolate cakes with petal toppings and coconut shavings.
"I never want to leave here," I tell Delilah. "This is where I'm meant to be. There's so much energy here."
"This is where we'll always come back to. Right here." Delilah says. "Once we're successful, we'll find a glamorous two-bedroom loft overlooking Central Park. We'll eat Chinese food at 2 AM and dance crazily at all the new clubs. It'll be amazing."
We flew home the next morning, still buzzing from the excitement of the city and the bottles of vodka we snuck from the hotel refrigerator the night before. Back home,

life was a blur. School was becoming unbearable. The preppies, as I nicknamed them, were too much. I craved New York. Delilah had signed up for an art class at our local college. When she wasn't there, she was obsessing over her latest project and her new classmates.

"They are so Zen," she gushes. "I feel like I can show these people my work and not be judged on its character." "That's great. I'm happy for you." We were sitting on our bench outside of the cafeteria, and I was contemplating ditching the rest of the day, as she showed me a new piece she was working on.

I don't tell her about the numerous emails from Edward. His emails bordering on flirtatious, he kept reminding me of the work we were creating and how my contribution was such a huge part. That I should seriously consider relocating to New York. With my birthday and graduation next month, it would be legal. But would Delilah come with me? And if she didn't…could I really leave her behind?

CHAPTER 7
BEGINNINGS OF CHAOS

Our book officially launched the beginning of May. Two first class tickets, we flew in style back to New York to celebrate our success. Friday night, we mingled with editors, writers, and movie critics. Everyone who was everyone was there. The room was elegantly decorated with dark purple drapes and silver centerpieces. Women dressed up as fairies with their sparkling skin and gauzy wings served hors-d'oeuvres and drinks. It reminded me of the gothic fairy tales I loved so much.

Delilah's hair was pinned with rhinestone clips, and curly tendrils fell from her eyes as she nervously shook hands with everyone. I was wearing a red strapless dress and my long dark hair flowing behind me. Squeezing my arm, Delilah squeals "I'm so nervous!"

"I know, right?! It's so beautiful in here!" I say admiring everyone in the room with their sparkly drinks and labels of fashion.

Four hours of awestruck later, we had mingled with the finest of the publishing world and were a little tipsy from the glasses of champagne that we had stolen.

"Well, ladies... I do believe this was a success," Edward says, winking at me as he chauffeured us to our car. As my stomach twisted in knots, I told myself that it was just a mixture of champagne and excitement.

CHAPTER 8
FRIENDS FOREVER

"The Urban Goddess" was a success. A success that threw us into the fast lane as books flew off the shelves and book signings were an everyday occurrence. Delilah was uncomfortable with all the attention. The hustle and bustle of the city scared her. She usually smiled timidly while signing her name, letting me do most of the chatting.

Not that I minded. I was loving every second of our success and wanted more. It was our last day in New York before flying home for a few weeks.

We were sitting at a coffee shop eating croissants and drinking caramel macchiatos. "So, I've been thinking," I begin.

"Yeah?" Delilah says looking up from her coffee.

"We've been going back and forth so much, and it's becoming exhausting. New York is so amazing. This is where the prosperity is. The business. The culture. I've made the decision to move here. Will you come with me?" I ask.

She stares out into the street and sighs.

"I love you, Jade. I love what we created. I do eventually want to get out of the town we're in and be somewhere else. But, I don't think New York is it. I thought it was, but it isn't. I want to be somewhere where it's quiet. Where I can plant lilies and tulips in my windows. I want to gaze upon my garden of lavender, mint, and tomatoes while I sip raspberry lemonade. I want to put sunflowers in my hair and paint in the sun. I'll never leave you and will visit you as much as I can. But I can't move here with you," she says solemnly.

"I understand," I tell her. "We'll never be apart." I grab her hand, holding onto the hope that she might be right. Jade and Delilah forever

CHAPTER 9
LOST GIRL

Here I am. Thirty-four years old with two kids and boyfriend will not get off his ass and work. I used to be beautiful. Blonde hair with streaks of gray from stress. There are lines upon my face from worry and the effects of too many cigarettes. Delilah looks just like I did as a teenager. Although, I was wild and she is so reserved. I guess that's why I let her do her own thing. Maybe you

could call me neglectful, but getting pregnant at sixteen...
I lost my childhood. I never got to be young and care-free.
Is it so bad that I want to do that now? And now she's
published a book with that little friend of hers. Do you
think she offered to help her mother in any way? As I sit
here in our small two-bedroom house with bare walls and
no furniture, I'm sure you can guess. I can't help but think
what a selfish brat she is as I button my uniform and head
to the diner for work. She's in the real world now. She's
going find out very quickly it's not all a fairy tale with a
handsome prince at the end. Sometimes it's about the
backseat of a car getting yourself knocked up at sixteen
and wishing every day you could just go back.

CHAPTER 10
CHANGES

It's been three weeks since I told Jade I wouldn't move
to the city with her. I miss her terribly. My art class keeps
me busy, but the darkness of the night reminds me that my
best friend is gone. I never really felt like I had a family.
My father abandoned us when I was five, and my mom has
tried to find a replacement ever since. Not one to ever be
alone, she jumps from guy to guy. My sister's father. She's
been with him the longest, and he's the worst of the worst.
Maybe that's why I feel so connected to Jade. She's
become my family. My only true family.

When I saw her last week, I could already see the
change. Jade, who has always been fashionable and daring,
walked into our coffee shop wearing dark skinny jeans and
Manolo Blahnik heels. Her flowy top was pale yellow, and
she had a Michael Kors bag around her shoulder. She was
beautiful but changed. She talked about all the new people
she had met at our publishing company. Raving about the
galleries she had visited, and the endless parties.
"So, how are you?!" she asked breathlessly.
"I'm good. My art class is going well. I'm learning so many

techniques that I never knew about," I tell her.

"That's great. I would love to see them." She asks me about going to a party later. It's an after party for a movie premiere she tells me.

"I don't know. I thought about visiting some museums and galleries."

"I'll make you a deal," Jade tells me. "If you go to the party with me later, we'll spend the day visiting whatever you like. Pleeasseee?!"

I relent.

We take a taxi to the Museum of Modern Art. Jade seems bored as we walk through each portrait. Tears welling up in my eyes, I'm so overwhelmed by the beauty of it all.

"Isn't it beautiful?" I tell her.

"It's lovely. I've been here a few times with some colleagues from the company," she tells me.

I grab her hand as we go to the next painting, her phone starts vibrating.

"It's Edward. I've been working for them. Helping with ideas and editing. They need me at the party by six. We need to go get ready."

Her apartment is small but cozy. Brick walls with her favorite pictures from home hanging. Flowing turquoise curtains hang from her windows, and her black futon is covered with pillows and books. Rummaging through her closet, she is looking for something to wear.

"Do you have a dress you can wear to the party?" she asks me. I pull out a long green maxi dress with flowers embroidered along the bottom. "I have this." I show her. "Umm… it's really pretty… but I think you need something a little fancier for this party."

She hands me a black dress with crisscross straps. It's fitted, and I feel like I'm on display. Jade lines my eyes with eyeliner and applies a burgundy lipstick to my lips. I don't recognize myself as I consider her bathroom mirror. She grabs my hand as we walk along the neon-lit streets, cool and confident.

The party is in full swing. Large screens on all four walls are playing previews from the movie. The bar is lit up with neon lights, and cocktail waitresses zip through the crowds with drinks. Velvet couches are positioned in each corner of the room, and the darkness is only lit up from the blaring movie screens. She slides onto one of the couches pulling me down with her.

A young guy with long blonde hair and ripped jeans is sitting in the middle of the couch smiling at us. "You must let me buy you two exquisite creatures a drink," he says, leaning in towards Jade.

"You're Jett Anders," Jade tells him.

"Beautiful and attentive," he says. "And you are?"

"I'm Jade," she says sweetly. "This is my friend, Delilah."

Briefly taking his eyes off Jade's chest, he looks over at me. "Nice to meet you, Delilah. Do you ladies live in the city?"

"I do. I just moved here. Delilah lives back in our hometown."

"Hmm... well... what do you say if we get out of here? I'm having a party at my house, and you can never have enough beautiful ladies surrounding you."

Jade looks at me with pleading eyes. "You go," I tell her. "I must be at the airport at 9. I can get a taxi to your place."

"No, I don't want to leave you." She grabs my hand.

"Jade... go. It's okay," I tell her.

Kissing me on the cheek, she whispers "I love you." They leave together with his arm around her waist as she stares up at him with her boy crush eyes and goofy grin.

CHAPTER 11
LEATHER PANTS AND LOVE

Parties. Fame. Money. Drugs. It's an all-inclusive package of being a celebrity. New York was becoming boring. Maybe it was time to move back to L.A. Or maybe not.

She walked in holding hands with a young, blonde girl who looked uncomfortable as hell. And when she slid down next to me, I could feel my heart beating. I've gotten so used to women falling over me, and I've fucked too many to count. But there was something different about her. She seemed to love the fact that I was a rocker, and the façade was something I was used to, so I went with it. She seemed genuinely interested in what I had to say. Running her fingers through my long hair and telling me about her book she just published. I told her about the early days when I was just starting out and how it felt to be on top of the world.

She wanted so badly to be accepted and part of this circle, that when I offered her the needle, she shyly asked me to do it. Why I did it, I don't know. Maybe I just wanted someone to be as fucked up as I am so I wouldn't be so lonely. As she rocked her hips slowly above me and I caressed the paleness of her skin, I knew I was hooked. She had become another drug that I was too weak to break

CHAPTER 12
JADED JADE

I'm packing up the last of my clothes when I hear the deadbolt turn. Jade walks in barefoot and her makeup smeared. She looks like she hasn't slept.
"Hey. I wanted to go with you to the airport," she says. She keeps fidgeting and twisting her hair around her fingers.
"Are you okay?" I ask her. She seems off.

"I'm fine. Just tired."

She looks at me for the first time and asks if I'm ready to go. Underneath the smudges of her black eyeliner, her pupils are wide and dilated. The color of hazel is almost completely gone.

"Are you high?" I ask her.

"It's fine. Jett and I really connected. He had so many ideas. He thinks I would be great at producing movies."

I'm suddenly fed up with it all. Jade. This city. Everything. "You're fucking high, Jade! Is this the success we worked so hard for? For you to go home with celebrities and do drugs? We were supposed to be in this together. And I've lost you. Lost you to the glitz and glamour of this jaded city. I guess you fit in now."

I left her there crying. Running her fingers up and down her skin, trying to ignore the drugs that were running through her veins.

CHAPTER 13
FAME AND FRENZY

The perks of being famous always seem more fabulous than what they are. The cars, the money, the notoriety.... it's amazing. But it always comes at a price. They never tell you about the pressure, the drugs, or the cost of having everyone know your name.

After our fight, Delilah refused my calls. Bouquets of flowers that I sent to her were never responded. The only notification from her was a new contract with her name voided from all aspects of our project. Her lack of response was like a punch in the gut. I felt sick over what had become of us. But the shimmering light of the celebrity world had given me tunnel vision. I could not see anything else.

Work was going well, and I was learning so much about the publishing world. "Jade, can you come into my office for a moment?" Edward asked me, motioning to me.

"So, we think you've been doing a great job. As you already know, everyone loves the book. It's sold out in the U.S. and has gone public worldwide. But, we think this can go bigger." He smiles.

"How much bigger are we talking? Like, making another book?" I ask.

"Maybe eventually we can have a part two. But there's a very reputable company who is considering making your book into a movie series."

"OMG! Really?!"

"Calm down...it's nothing official right now. Just talking about the possibility of it. It looks promising. Keep up the good work, kiddo." He winks.

I walk out of his office, and I begin to wonder. What are dreams without possibility? What was life without a little chaos? I felt like one of those snow globes you find in a novelty store. Easily broken but beautiful. Shaking it within your hands to see the snow spinning around you. Waiting for the moment when everything settles down and it is still again. But there's always that urge. The urge to turn your life upside with the snow whirling around you.

<u>CHAPTER 14</u>
A HARDENED HEART

Just as I expected, "The Urban Goddess" was a hit. Edward Johnston is never wrong about these things. When it comes to success and money, it's a cutthroat business. Jade seems to be handling the fame very well. I can appreciate the tight, little dresses she wears in the office. She told me her friend was uncomfortable in the spotlight and decided to back out. That's price of stardom. You either fly, or you fall. Relationships are always broken in the process.

Maybe I should offer a lending ear if she needs it. Women love that shit. She doesn't seem to be responding to anything else. Maybe she thinks I'm an arrogant asshole.

She would be right. I wasn't always this way. An unhappy marriage, too much scotch, and the power to crush someone's dream will turn you into a monster dressed in an Armani suit.

CHAPTER 15
CHARCOAL HANDS

I miss her. Two girls with dreams and aspirations. Black onyx and aquamarine. Drastically different but so exquisite together. She has faded into the night, and I'm still here…struggling to find myself within this storm of heartbreak and loneliness.

I dream of a place where lilies and violets bloom. Rolling hills and shady trees that dance in the breeze. A cottage with front porch swings. Mending my garden in bare feet as my dress ripples in the wind. Not that I believe there is such a place. For they only exist in the fairy tales that Jade and I had imagined.

In my art class the next day, I saw him sitting by the window with charcoal in his hand and a faraway stare. Long brown hair pulled back into a ponytail, his green eyes were hidden behind dark-rimmed glasses. He was busy sketching as he listened to the teacher talk about our next project. Distracted, I accomplished nothing besides infatuation.

After class, he walks up to me extending his hand. "Hi. I'm Aiden."

"Delilah… did you just sign up?" I ask him as I take his hand.

"Yeah. Moved here with my dad. He's stationed here."

"Oh, nice. Well, I hope you liked the class and I'll see you on Wednesday."

"You will," he says, handing me a rolled-up paper.

He walked off before I could ask what it was. I opened it up, gasping. Perfectly etched in charcoal was a portrait of me. My hair was around my face, and I was staring at my desk. I must have been worrying as I usually do because there was despair in my eyes. But he made it beautiful. He made me beautiful.

CHAPTER 16
NEW BEGINNINGS

After mom died, my dad transferred here for a fresh start. Living in our old house was too much for him to bear. Not that we ever stayed in one place very long. But she had died in that light, blue bedroom with him beside her, and it haunted him every night. So here we are. I decided to take a year off before college. Dad didn't say much. He never does. I look just like her. My green eyes remind him of her. Even hidden behind my glasses, he cannot look at me. His job keeps him busy, and he's gone for training a lot. I decided to enroll in an art class to keep me busy in between job hunting.

That's where I saw her. She was sitting there with her hair surrounding her face like a fortress. You could tell her mind was somewhere else. The sketch did not do her justice, as she kept looking up and over at me. I didn't want to come off as creepy, as I tend to do sometimes. I've never been very good at talking to girls, so I usually just become intrigued from afar. I spent the entire class telling myself to not be a chicken shit and give her the picture. It seemed to go well. She was even more beautiful up close. I hope she likes it. Hoping she likes me.

CHAPTER 17
HALF OF MY HEART

I truly believe that we are put in places for a reason. Certain people come into your life when you need it most. To give a glimmer of light in your world of darkness. After that first day, Aiden and I became inseparable. I'm so scared to let my guard down, but he is so patient. He gives me peace. He gives me the companionship I had longed for and so much more. But through the comfort of his arms and the taste of his kiss, I still missed her. My other half. Jade and Delilah. Would I ever see her again? Was she ever real? Or had I imagined my goddess friend within my mind? Jade. Hecate. My wild indigo flower.

CHAPTER 18
LIGHTS.CAMERA.ACTION.

Living in Manhattan could make you feel like there was no other place besides there. Losing yourself into the burgundy leaves of Central Park. The neon lights with billboard women with their pouty lips and perfect hair. Everything you could think of was here. Maybe it was too much. Maybe that's how it pulled you in. But once you were in could you ever get out?

After months of hellish exhaustion and rehearsals, "The Urban Goddess" finally met cinema. It was all so surreal. The bright lights, producers, and stick thin models who wanted to be actresses. Attending movie premieres in slinky dresses and cosmopolitans was a typical Friday night. This was the life I had wanted. Jett's hands were around my waist as we walked through another party. The room was decorated with white walls and red tapestries. The lights were dimmed against the black carpeting. "C'mon baby, let's check out the VIP room," he says nuzzling my neck.

We walk into the darkened room where there are canopy beds covered in gold blankets. Maroon and purple pillows are stacked on top, and people are lounging on top of them, glazed and stoned. Jett pulls up his sleeve that uncovers the track marks on his arm. He wraps a tourniquet around his arm and sticks the needle into his vein. His eyes roll back, and he starts smiling, rubbing the spot where he injected.

"C'mon baby, it's your turn," he says pulling me towards

him.

I remove the velvet gloves that cover my arms. There are small, purple bruises sprinkled along my skin. I never inject myself. He always does it for me. I tell myself it's not really an addiction if I don't do it to myself. That familiar euphoria comes over me. I fade off into the darkness where I dream of desert skies and Delilah beside me. But it never lasts. The elation fades, and the craving begins. How long do I lie there on that bed catatonic? What only feels like moments are months. A drug infested zombie with a Manhattan loft and celebrity boyfriend. Jade. A violet flower girl who has wilted within the neon lights and the poisons that run through her.

<u>CHAPTER 19</u>
BOY.MAN.ROCKER.

She has her arm around my waist, and I pull her closer to me, smelling her perfume. The scent of her hair. I love her, but I've destroyed her. Just like I destroy everything I touch. But I cannot stop. She was now beside me as we drive 100 mph down the highway with no seatbelts on. It was only a matter of time before we crashed. Just when I think I've gathered the strength to stop for the both of us, I find us lying there, entranced and drugged. A needle in my hand and venom running through our veins.
Did she love me back? They never loved me for me, but for what I was.

It was different with Jade. She was the one I wanted, the only one. Without the fame, the money, or the drugs that drained her, she would eventually leave. Eventually, she'd see I was just an insecure boy who happened to play guitar and looked good in leather pants. If she ever left, I'm not sure I could handle it. I wasn't always this way. I used to be really shy before my mom started putting me in commercials as a kid. She was your typical stage-mom. Frosted blonde hair and big tits, she would smile for the directors; wooing them with her low-cut dresses and charm. When she realized that commercials weren't going to fund the life she wanted, we moved to L.A. where she sent me to auditions for movies and boy bands. I was picked up by a talent agent at fifteen and joined The West Coast Boys, a boy band with choreographed dance moves and love songs too sappy for a fifteen-year-old kid.

She loved it. She loved the attention. And most of all, the money. She blew everything I ever made. Mansions, her BMW, plastic surgery to make her waist invisible and her lips bee-stung pouty. At eighteen, I had made millions. But, I had nothing to show for it. Finally realizing that she only cared about the money, and not me, I left. I deserted The West Coast Boys and went rogue. I hitchhiked around the U.S. for months, writing.

My hair was long, and tattoos inked across my body I was nothing like the boy from before. I was a man. I founded Tortured Soul, finally creating work that I wanted. I send her money from time to time to keep her off my ass. I can see her sitting there with her martini glass, slurring her words into the phone as she orders from QVC.

Boy band chicks are so different from rocker chicks. Teeny-boppers are teary and emotional, sharing their selfies online. Rocker chicks will sit on your lap, caressing your knee as they whisper dirty words into your ear. I lived the life well. Sex, money, and rock n roll. Touring the world with a groupie on my arm and every drug you could ever imagine.

After a while, it wears you down. You give in. You inject. You become another lifeless soul with celebrity stamped across your forehead.

CHAPTER 20
BEHIND CLOSED DOORS

It's becoming unbearable. I want so badly to stop, but I can't. At eighteen years old, I've accomplished more than some people do their whole lives. How did this dream turn into a nightmare? I have this man. This beautiful, talented man. And he's a junkie. I am one too now. I let the taste of his kiss and his piercing eyes turn me into an addict.

We look like the perfect couple. Fake smiles and laughter that hide my tears. Behind closed doors, it's us in the dark. Lying there beside him as I ponder my own life. Picking him up off the floor because he's passed out from the drugs. Those are the moments of fame that are hidden beneath the red-carpet gowns and the camera lights that shine upon my face. I'm sitting on my balcony wrapped in a blanket even though it's summertime. I've lost so much weight from stress and the perpetual size zero of couture fashion, that I stay cold constantly.

He's inside pacing. Running his fingers through his hair as he screams at his manager through the phone. He's fiending. Yearning for that pinch of pain that blinds your suffering, sending you into a frenzy of comatose bliss.

CHAPTER 21
I DREAM OF A LIFE

"I want to leave here," I tell Aiden as he lies on the hood of his car, eating fruit and Hawaiian bread. "Promise me that we'll leave this place one day. Go far away. A bungalow with wooden floors. Blue skies as far as you can see. And when it rains, we'll catch raindrops with our tongues. Eating fruit salads with whip cream and forgetting the craziness that this world has become." "Wherever you go, I will be with you. You are my home," he says, cupping my chin and kissing me on the lips. I can taste the sweetness of strawberries. The pieces of my heart that are slowly unbreaking.

After I left New York and signed our project over to Jade, I never expected anything from it. But every month an envelope arrived with money inside. A small card with Jade's initials and no return address. I never spent it. Stashing it away, I figured that if I could hide the money, I could hide how it had destroyed us.

A week later when her letter arrived, there was no money. Only a plane ticket to a small town in upstate New York. I hid the ticket along with the money, unsure if I wanted to go. Aiden told me he supported whatever decision I made, but maybe I needed the closure. My heart was finally mending, I wasn't sure if I could handle it unraveling again.

I borrowed Aiden's car, and I drove to the mountain lodge where Jade and I first stayed when we created Andromeda. I drank peppermint schnapps hot chocolates, and I ate bagels with blueberry cream cheese. I found myself walking around town, window shopping at bookstores and little ma' and pa' shops.

There was a park at the edge of town where you could walk along the nature trails. Mountains of snow surrounding me, there were small patches of grass that were trying to unbury themselves. Stopping to take a few pics of the scenery, I see it. A small purple flower. Winter heath. Alone and vibrant against the paleness of the snow, standing strong against the harshness of the earth. It was Jade.

CHAPTER 22
HOUSE OF HEALING

Armed with my carry-on bag and plane ticket, I find my seat next to the window. I've flown so much since our debut, but I cannot get used to it. My ears never pop, and I hate the flip-flop feeling in my stomach as we ascend. For two hours, I stare out at the clouds trying to figure everything out. With no official address, I had no idea where I was going. I walk into baggage claim, and I see an older gentleman with gray hair holding up a sign with my name on it.

"Hi, I'm Delilah," I say.

"Pleasure to meet you, Delilah. I'm William. Do you have any other bags?" he asks.

"Just a small suitcase."

He grabs my bag off the conveyer belt and escorts me to a black van that is waiting by the curb. He gets into the driver seat and starts up the engine.

"Where exactly are we going? Do you know Jade?" I ask.

"Jade and I have become very well acquainted. She's doing okay." He smiles into the rearview mirror.

We drive out of the city into the countryside. We turn into a long gravel road, and I see an old Victorian style house with dark red shutters and a wrap-around porch. Weeping willow trees surround the house, and there are people walking along the meadow of flowers that meet you as you turn in. We pull up to the front porch, and there is a wooden sign that says "Artemis, House of Healing." Jade is sitting in a large wicker chair wearing dark sunglasses.

"I'm so glad you are here," she says wrapping her arms around me. I start to cry. I cry for the time we spent apart. For the bruises on her arms that were still healing. For the frailty of her body as I squeezed her back. She was still beautiful. Her dark hair still long and flowing. Her eyes sunken in underneath her glasses, but the hazel still shone brightly. She looked so sick but so radiant.

"Walk with me," she says, grabbing my hand. We walk through the meadow of sunflowers. Lifting my face towards the warmth of the sun, Jade pins flowers into my hair.

We don't talk much. It's as if we don't have to. Her room was on the second floor and reminded me of her bedroom back home. Her pictures hung above her bed, and there were her favorite literary quotes written in red lipstick across her mirror.

There are rows of unopened pill bottles on the bedside table. "I know I can never go back and undo everything I did to you," she says. "I let fame and money get in the way of what was important. I was too busy looking for something else to realize what I already had. You were right. I had become so jaded. I let someone take my light. And now the candle is burning at both ends. I don't want to just lie here before it burns out completely. I want to live before I die. I'm so sorry, Delilah." Tears rim her eyes.

"We are Jade and Delilah. Two halves that make a whole. My soul sister. I forgive you," I tell her.

She smiles at the ceiling, closing her eyes. "One last adventure."

CHAPTER 23
LIVE OR DIE

I still remember the exact moment when I knew that if I didn't leave, this would bury me alive. Screaming in the darkness as I slowly suffocated within my own self. Two A.M. in his penthouse suite, I shook uncontrollably as the drugs he injected in me ran rampant. Stumbling towards his balcony, contemplating whether I should jump or not. I don't remember exactly how long I sat there, but I could hear a voice telling me to get up. A girl's voice. I could feel her hair along my cheek, smelling of lavender and mint. She was with me that night. Holding me up as I walked out of the darkness and into the light.

Two weeks in the hospital, detoxing, was a living nightmare. Dying had to better than this. Lying there sweating, scraping my fingernails against my skin. Feeling the imaginary bugs that ran through my blood, I could see a tiny glimpse of hope. Hoping that I would make it out alive. And I did.

I'm now drug-free and seeing the world for its true beauty. But it will never be enough. I signed my own death certificate. Here I am, living dead.

But Delilah had come. My mother had visited when she could, but I would never leave with her. I couldn't bring myself to go back to the very place I had started. I remember reading in middle school that in Greek mythology, the Gods separated humans into two beings. So, they would spend eternity looking for their other half.

I often wondered if this was also meant for friends and not just lovers. I believe it. Delilah was my other half. I had found my best friend. My only friend. The one who accepted my gothic, mythical, hellish personality…and loved me anyway.

Resting on my bed with the wind on our faces, I told her I wanted to go home.

"Where do you want to go?" she asks.

"Wherever home is to you. Because you're my home. I'm just sorry it took me so long to figure that out."

I would miss New York. There were adventures that were happy, and it was also a place of sadness. Even though I was on borrowed time, it had given me my life back. For the first time, I planned on living it.

CHAPTER 24
BREAKING NEWS

She is gone. I could not keep her. I ruined her spirit with liquid malice. Her body withered and tired, she found the strength to leave. I am alone. Always alone. Where else is there to go? Nowhere. I drown my sorrows with the burn of vodka and the numbness of pills melting on my tongue. Drifting off into the blackness, her picture in the palm of my hand.

Headlines printed: Lead singer, Jett Anders of Tortured Soul, Found Dead in his Penthouse Suite. Cause of death: Alcohol, Vicodin, and Heartbreak.

CHAPTER 25
GOODBYE, NEW YORK

During my week vacation, Jade had disappeared with no hint of her whereabouts. No notice or forwarding address. The only clue of her existence was a phone call from her attorney, calling to address the legalities of her contract. I will miss her. Not for just the tight dresses and cleavage, but she was a spunky kid. She never fell into the bullshit I fed her. The life of fame is too much for some. Or maybe she got out before it got too bad. Wherever she is, I wish her well.

CHAPTER 26
HOME

I brought Jade home. I took her to the small cottage that Aiden and I bought together. Wooden floors and pale yellow walls. Pictures of our artwork framed along the hallway and the windows were always open. Fruit baskets along the kitchen counters, and a large couch covered with fleece blankets and pillows. Aiden had painted Jade's room purple and sketched pictures of us that he hung above her bed. I hadn't realized until I saw him, how much I had missed him. The familiar scent of his embrace, he hugged me tightly before turning to Jade.

"So, this is the one who has stolen your heart," she says grinning.

"Which half?" he asks. She smiles at him for a moment before I realize she is on the verge of tears. Squeezing our hands, she tells us she's ready for home.

"I'm pretty beat from the trip. You mind if I take a nap?" she asks.

"No, go ahead. I'm going to make dinner in a bit." Aiden puts her bags in her room, and I watch her standing at the doorway for a few moments before closing the door.

"I missed you so much," I tell him, burying my face

into his chest.

"I missed you too." He kisses my forehead.

We start dinner while Jade sleeps. Spaghetti squash and strawberry shortcake. Fresh from the garden we had grown in our backyard. Cutting up the strawberries, he asks "Do they know how far it's progressed?"

"Not yet. She has an appointment on Monday. They will know whether it's just the virus, or if it has advanced on."

He wraps his arms around me, as the tears flow down my cheeks. For all the strength that Jade possessed, I knew deep down this was stronger.

CHAPTER 27
DIAMOND TEARS

It wasn't until Delilah arrived home with Jade did I realize how much she meant to her. And how sick Jade truly was. Her body small and bony, dark circles that surrounded her hazel eyes.

Watching my mother die, I knew it was coming. I saw their closeness, their bond. I help out when I can, but mostly let them have their time together. At night, she would crumple within my arms, her cries muffled into my chest. During the day, she was different. Strong. I could see why she loved Jade. She pushed Delilah to try new things. To take chances and let loose. They grounded each other.

I loved this girl with long, blonde hair and flowers pinned within her braid. The way she viewed our world, believing that everything was beautiful in its own way. I wanted to save her from this heartache, as I knew all too well the pain it brings. But I couldn't. All I can do is hold her close, as the strength from the day slowly crumbles into the night.

CHAPTER 28
LIVING DEAD

"Good Morning, Jade. I'm Dr. Martinez." She shakes my hand.

The lesions along my hands are covered with lace gloves, and I feel self-conscious touching her. Hoping that she doesn't find me as repulsive as I find myself.

"How are you feeling?" she asks.

"I'm just really tired, and I can't seem to shake this cough."

"We can try and give something for the cough, especially for at night. Home remedies such as chamomile tea can help soothe also. I got your lab results back this morning, and we need to go ahead to discuss everything while you're here."

Delilah grabs my hands and squeezes.

"Okay. What did it show?" I ask her.

"Unfortunately, we have now gotten to the point where it's progressed past just the virus. I'm very sorry to have to inform you of this, but the tests show you now have AIDS. We need to get you as healthy as possible. And on medication immediately."

"Even with medication, how long do I have?" I ask.

"There are patients that can live a long and relatively healthy life. Usually up to three years with proper medication. If you choose to do nothing, it's only a matter of time before your body shuts down."

"I don't want any drugs. I don't want to live the remainders of my days in the hospital or swallowing pills. I know that I did this to myself. And this is the price for my gambling. I'm ready to accept it."

"I strongly urge you to reconsider. There are many therapies and medications that can alleviate your symptoms. To give you some normality and strength. But if this is the path you want to take, we can get you hospice care when the time arrives to keep you comfortable."

Delilah is quiet. "Are you sure you don't want to try any of this?" she asks me.

"Yes. I spent too much time putting things into my body that I hated. I'm at peace with this. I wish it wasn't this way, but it is. I'm asking a lot. I understand if you cannot do it."

"You are my family, Jade. I don't want you to go. But I will be with you until the end."

I gaze upon my body in the mirror. The fullness of my breasts is gone, and my stomach has been hollowed out. You can see the outlines of my ribs that jut out beneath my clothes. Small, purple lesions cover my back. I feel like a skeleton corpse whose heart continues to beat. Afraid to show her the ugliness of this disease, I hide it underneath gauzy sweaters and silk scarves that I wrap around my head.

It wasn't until my strength was gone, did I finally relent. Holding onto her shoulders as she helped me undress and ease me into a warm bath. She was unafraid. Pouring warm water over my shoulders as I cried tears of appreciation, she hummed along with the running water. I sat there amongst the mixture of vanilla and jasmine, wondering what I did to deserve someone who loved me as much as she did.

CHAPTER 29
SOUL SISTERS

She is weak but strong. Scarred, but beautiful. Refusing my help, I let her be. Not wanting to take what independence she has left, I stand by watching her struggle.

It was a late summer night, and you could hear the crickets singing in the darkness. I hear her calling me softly from the bathroom.

"Jade, are you okay?"

"I can't do it," she sobs.

"It's okay, unlock the door. Let me help you."

I can hear her crying, but she doesn't open the door. "Jade, please. Are you okay?!"

She opens the door slowly. Her eyes are red from crying, and she's sitting on the tile floor with a towel wrapped around her. I put her arms around my shoulders and lift her slowly. Dropping her towel, I can see the marks on her back. Her bones protruding from her body. "I'm sorry," she says with tears in her eyes.

"You, my love, have nothing to be sorry for," I tell her. "I'm here from beginning to end. Soul sisters through thick and thin."

"Did you just make that up?" she asks giggling.

"It just occurred to me, thank you very much," I say matter-of-factly.

Her laughter was a brightness that shown for the first time in weeks. For a moment, she sounded like the old Jade. The girl with fire in her soul and inspiration in her heart. Her light was fading. A candle flickering in the wind, I stand over her sheltering her from the elements that will turn her into darkness.

Her health rapidly deteriorating, she grew weaker as the days passed. It wasn't until I found her limp on the bathroom floor did I persist that she could not battle this alone. I saw her lying there in that hospital bed. She looked so frail as IV fluids dripped into her veins. Waking in sporadic moments, she would smile as I sat next to her, reading her favorite stories.

"Delilah?" I hear a voice.

"Dr. Martinez again. Does Jade have any family we can contact? We need to speak to them immediately about Jade's condition."

"Jade did not want to include her mother in this. I am her family."

"Delilah, I understand that you are her friend—" she starts.

"No. You do not understand. I am her family. Her only

family. Whatever you need to say, you can say to me," I say firmly, trying to hide the tears welling up in my eyes. She smiled softly at me, as if appreciative of my anger.

"Jade's organs have begun to shut down. She is in kidney failure. We can keep her comfortable, but it won't be much longer. I'm very sorry."

I see her there, in a medicated trance. The beeping of machines humming along with each breath she took. Her voice replaying in my head to not let her die in a hospital. To let her go with dignity and the comfort of her bed. It was time to go home.

CHAPTER 30
SAYING GOODBYE

I held on for three months and five days. Each day, as I grew weaker, Delilah grew stronger. I spent my days on the front porch, writing and reading. Nibbling on fruit and pieces of bread that Delilah brought me.

On the good days, we walked along the meadows. Picking flowers for our hair and her teaching me to paint. I helped them mend the garden, feeling the coolness of the soil between my fingers. On the bad days, Delilah would wash my hair with her homemade lavender shampoo. Dabbing my skin with frankincense and eucalyptus, she prayed that these natural remedies would give me relief. Covering me with fleece blankets as we swung together on the porch swing.

I don't remember much of my days in the hospital. Took weak to comprehend my own demise. When I passed, even through the haze of painkillers, I felt her embrace. The scent of her shampoo. Her tears on my face that cleansed my soul. In my mind the places we visited. That snowy, little cottage. Our impromptu beach trips. Our coffee shop. And that stone bench where I first saw her that day. My urban gypsy friend, my real-life Persephone. Delilah.

CHAPTER 31
MY GLASS HEART

My heart is broken. She is gone. During her illness, the sicker she got, the more beautiful she became. But when the pain was too much, she finally relented for some relief. The haziness the drugs gave her made her euphoric. Passing on the wisdom of books, literature, and her time in New York. Recounting our days when the world was ours and we were still innocent to the perils of adulthood. Laughing about the adventures we had taken, and the stories we created.

We laid in her bed with my arms around her withered body. As the sun finally set into the night, it took Jade with him. "I love you, soul sister," I whispered, tears running down my cheeks. I stayed there all night with my arms around her, hoping that she wasn't really gone.

We brought her ashes to the mountains where we took our first trip. At the edge of the park where I had found the winter heath so long ago, we spread her ashes. A week after Jade's passing, I received a telegram from her lawyer. It stated in Jade's will that I was the executor of her estate, and to contact him immediately.

"I had no idea she had any estate," I tell Aiden.

"I'm not sure, babe. You should probably call her lawyer."

It took a few tries before finally getting a hold of her attorney.

"Delilah, hello. My name is Chris Samson, and I was Jade's attorney. I'm so sorry to hear about her passing. You have my condolences." He says.

"Thank you," I tell him solemnly.

"In her will, she has left you executor of her estate. She left her mom an undisclosed amount of money, but everything else has been left solely to you."

"What everything?" I ask.

"Jade sold her portion of the movie project to the

production company before she left New York. She also sold her New York apartment. She contacted me to set up her will and help with the legalities of her contract."

"How much was her portion and the apartment?" I ask.

"Her apartment sold for $100,000 and her compensation for the book and movie added up to five million dollars." He says.

"Are… are you saying this goes to me?" I gasp.

"Yes, ma'am, I am. We will need you to, of course, sign papers and take care of a few things she left behind, but this all goes to you. She also left a small lockbox that I will send you via UPS."

I am in complete awe. I've never been one that cared about having a lot of money. If I could paint, I was always content. Growing up less fortunate had made me humble, but Jade made sure that there would never be a need for anything. But it was more money than I would ever need. I donated part of it to charities that Jade had loved. I started a writing school in her name for young adults who wanted to write. No person turned away because they couldn't pay. They compensated with their passion for literature, and the stories they created.

A small, silver lockbox arrived two weeks later. I cried through the contents of that box. Inside were snapshots of our adventures. Beach pictures with our salty hair and tan lines. Our red noses as we walked along the snowy shops looking for inspiration. All our original stories and my paintings were tucked at the bottom. And a letter from Jade:

Dear Delilah,

I now know that by the time you receive this, I will be gone. Hopefully to a place where everyone is loved, and it's always sunny. I can spend my days writing on a cloud, waiting for the day when we're reunited. I will miss you, friend. But, remember to enjoy the life you've been given…and the only regret in life is not taking the occasional risk. Accept love, find inspiration, and always remember your worth. For we are two goddesses trying to find our way. You are the day to my night. Persephone and Hecate. Onyx and aquamarine. Jade and Delilah forever.

I framed her letter and set it on my bedside table. As time passes, so will the pain. Losing Jade was excruciatingly beautiful. To lose someone you love is one of the rawest moments in one's life. There are days where I succumb to the tears of my loss. Aiden has been my rock. Unbreaking my heart piece by piece, he has been my constant. I can sometimes smell her perfume as I pass her old bedroom, her curtain blowing in the breeze. I know she is with us. Her dark hair flowing against the wind and her hazel eyes sparkling with excitement as she asks me, "Are you ready for an adventure?"

~ABOUT THE AUTHOR~

Jessica Ashby is a second-time author who resides in Brownwood, TX. Born in North Carolina, she has traveled with her husband extensively through his military career, finally settling down in Texas. She has two bright and talented daughters and one son, who is both inquisitive and overwhelming adorable. In her spare time she enjoys reading, writing, and dancing. *The Beauty Within* is the title of Jessica's first published book.

www.ingramcontent.com/pod-product-compliance
Lightning Source LLC
Chambersburg PA
CBHW050914120626
46552CB00004B/1570